JEFFREY J. KILPATRICK

HOMETOWN HORRORS

TERRIFYING TALES OF ATHENS

Volume One:

BLOODY BOULEVARD

JEFFREY J. KILPATRICK

HOMETOWN HORRORS

TERRIFYING TALES OF ATHENS

Volume One:

BLOODY BOULEVARD

TABLE OF CONTENTS

AGAINST THE GRAIN

"The rough outer layer of pine spiraled in on itself, exposing the soft virgin heartwood beneath, the wood's true form freed from its captivity by the sharp steel blade of the vintage Stanley C559B jack bench plane. Once oppressive fibers vacated their stronghold, fleeing before the assault of the righteous blade. Lines broken, the insolent speckled tyrants fell to the floor in defeat, testaments of futility."

Sharon smiled. Woodworking always made her think in aureate prose. Testaments of futility. She liked that one. She drew one finger along the fresh cut, unconcerned. The blade was beyond sharp; there would be no splinters here.

"Excellent work, Sharon."

Gabe. Sharon felt the heat rise up her neck at the sound of his voice.

"Oh, thanks," she replied.

"No, really," continued Gabe. "You're showing great control of your tools. Good pressure, smooth form. Really excellent."

God, her cheeks were on fire now. She hoped nobody else in the studio was watching.

"I think you're ready for our advanced class."

"Oh, I don't know about that."

"You should consider it. Smaller class—only about four or five—and a really great group."

Sharon nodded vaguely, concentrating on her work.

"Promise me you'll think about it?"

His hand was resting just next to hers. An involuntary twitch of the finger and they would be touching. Gabe's eyes flashed to the back of the room. Another student was having trouble getting his chisel to work at the correct angle.

"Okay, yes. Sure," Sharon stammered. She was flustered. This was the longest conversation they had ever had.

"Great."

Gabe turned to go, his hand brushing against her wrist. A wave of goosebumps raced up her arm.

"I think you need that class, Sharon. I really do."

Sharon exhaled. She couldn't remember breathing at all during that whole exchange. A dark smear had formed on the wood plank where her hand had been. Sweat. Good grief, she

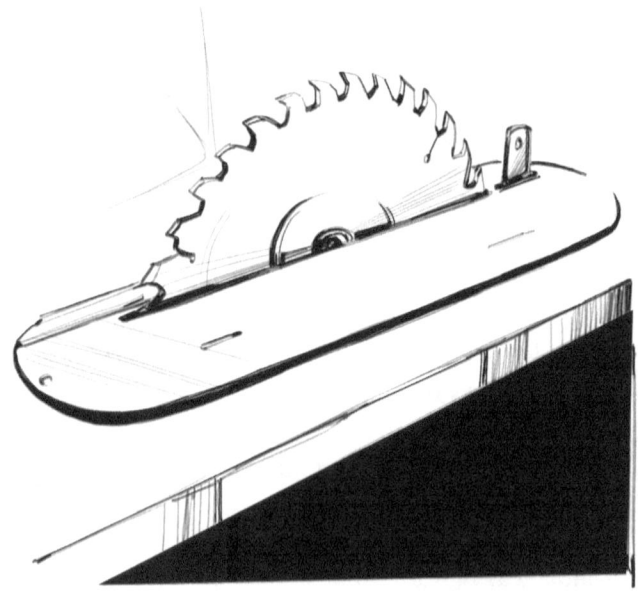

was a wreck. The woman at the next work bench gave her a curt nod, followed by raised eyebrows and a wry smile.

"What happens at Oneta Woodworks stays at Oneta Woodworks, eh, June?" she said to her friend at the next bench, louder than Sharon thought necessary.

"Sounds about right," said another woman two rows over. Sharon caved inward, goosebumps replaced by the dry itchiness of embarrassment. They *had* been watching. *You're such a fool, Sharon. A right idiot.* She scooped up her plane and reshelved it. She swept up the scraps from the floor, tidied up her work station as quickly as she could, and left.

Outside in the cool air, she regained her composure. The sun was low in the sky, softening the harsh lines of the back view of the Chase Street Warehouses across the street. She liked this part of Athens. It felt hidden, undiscovered. She walked slowly to her car as usual, never in a big hurry to get home. This was her time. "Sharon's hour," she called it. Back home, it would all begin again.

And so it did.

Sharon quietly crept into the kitchen where a sour odor tinged her nose.. The TV was on full volume in the back room; talking heads shouting back and forth at each other about water regulations.

He can't even take out the trash, that oaf.

She checked the faded rooster wall clock: 5:12. Still enough time to put the steaks in the oven and at least get the water boiling. Sharon whirled around the room like a practiced sous-chef. Oven on, pot filled, steaks trimmed and seasoned, pot covered and set on high heat, steaks in the oven. 5:19, still time to get the rice going. Sharon slid the stool over to the pantry and mounted it before it came to a stop. Top shelf, third from the left. Reaching up, her wrist grazed the outstretched flap of a half-open box of Cheerios. It sent a shiver up her arm. Goosebumps. Gabe.

She drew her arm back on instinct, but her ring caught on the protruding metal of the rice jar's clasp. It fell. Shards of glass careened across the pantry floor and into the kitchen, and the rice followed, trickling under the stacks of newspaper and into the large seam of the kitchen threshold. Everywhere. The floor was awash in a sea of rice and glass.

Sharon paused, froze really. The mumbled voices from the TV in the back room droned on with indifference. No change. She stepped off the stool and grabbed the broom, crunching the rice and glass beneath her. Shoving the stool to the side, she started sweeping. In a moment she had a small pile collected in the dustpan. The water was boiling now, frantically bouncing the lid on the pot. She moved to take the lid off and paused again, staring down at the frenetic water.

It's controlled confusion. Anarchy.

The bubbles rose and burst in the cooler air, tumbling over each other, fighting for space. She tilted the dustpan, hand shaking.

You should do it, Sharon.

The thin plastic corner teetered on the lip of the pot, just above the chaos. A smattering of grains spilled into the pot.

How far would that buffalo of a man get into his meal before he found that sliver of glass behind his gums? How long before he realized that all the bites before it had been the same?

She emptied the dustpan. Furry strings of bubbles floated up off the glass like clear beaded necklaces. It was exquisite. She wanted to twirl the strands around her fingers, lace them up her wrists like jewelry, embrace the bedlam, wear it with honor.

Sharon reached down into the pot. Her fingers were inches from the water when a large piece of glass exploded. Drops of

scalding water peppered her shoulders and neck like ant bites. A second explosion. Sharon pushed the pot back off the flame, spilling it over the top of the stove. She reeled back against the far wall. Steam spewed out of the small gap between the counter and the stove.

What were you thinking?

Sharon collapsed, hugging her shoulders in a solo embrace. Her mind clouded with anger, and horror. And pity. She huddled further into the corner, bringing her knees up into a seated fetal position. Pity. She felt the shadow fall over her eyes, the darkness that always came to take her away.

This wasn't what I wanted.

She closed her eyes, not wanting to watch as the room shrank to a pinpoint and she was pulled back into the silence.

I'm so sorry.

In the back room, the continual murmur of the TV rambled on.

"Oneta Woodworks prides itself on craftsmanship. Perhaps more important than our own skills, though, are the skills of our students."

Gabe stood at the front of the class, beard trimmed, flannel shirt tucked in behind his wide leather belt. Sharon noted how he only tucked when he was presenting or lecturing. As this was the exhibition, it was an obvious tuck-in day.

"You five are the first advanced class that we have had. I'm going to be honest, the next group has some big toolboxes to fill. In the past six weeks, you have created some really incredible work."

Sharon and the other four shared a communal glance of pride. Behind them, family members and invited guests stood waiting patiently.

"So, take your time," continued Gabe. "Have a look around, and feel free to ask our students any questions you might have. I think y'all will agree, here at Oneta Woodworks, we really can build you anything."

There was a round of appreciative applause before the crowd dispersed into their various cohorts, parents and spouses gathering around their respective loved-ones' tables. Sharon lingered for a moment, then ducked out onto the loading dock. No one was here for her. Besides, she had chosen not to put her project in the show. It wasn't in her nature. With woodworking she was in control, she was the master, she had the power. Putting up her work for others to judge and ridicule would ruin that feeling; tear down that flimsy facade of confidence. Besides, this piece was too personal. Nobody would have understood.

It's better this way.

"You know, I couldn't say this in front of everyone," said a voice from behind Sharon, snapping her back to the present.

Gabe. Sharon's spine tensed into a rigid stilt, propping her up above her suddenly shaky legs.

"Your work really is superior. The best in the class."

Sharon managed to turn her head in his direction.

"Oh?"

"By far. Too bad we didn't get to see the finished product, the detail in the individual pieces is first-rate."

He turned her towards him. Sharon had to focus on locking her knees to keep herself upright. She hoped she didn't pass out.

"I notice he's not here tonight."

Sharon frowned, confused. Gabe indicated her ring finger, her bare ring finger.

"Oh. Yes, I decided, um, well, he's not here."

"That's what I said. Never is, is he? And now you've taken off the ring. Something change?"

Sharon turned away. She wasn't expecting this, wasn't ready yet.

You'll never be ready again. Never.

Gabe stood in awkward silence for a moment, shuffling his feet in the errant lines of sawdust.

"Look, I'm sorry. Too much."

Sharon nodded.

"Maybe I could help you take your work home. It's heavy, and I have a truck."

Sharon nodded again.

"Great. I'll load it up and meet you back out here in five."

Sharon watched him bound up the stairs.

You're an idiot, Sharon. Don't bring him to the house.

Maybe she should, though. Maybe this was how it was supposed to be, maybe she needed his help to move on. Really move on.

A dark red pickup pulled up, long planks of engraved wood peeking up above the bed. Her project. They drove in silence to the house. When they parked, Sharon got out and unlocked the front door. Gabe lowered the gate of the truck, wrestled the planks onto the dolly, and followed her inside.

A fetid air of rot ballooned out from the interior of the house. Gabe struggled to maintain the dolly with one hand as he covered his nose with the other. Sharon looked sheepish.

"Sorry. The trash needs to go out."

Gabe waved her off.

"No problem. I work next to the chicken plant, remember?"

Sharon wedged the door open to the living room.

"Maybe put it in here?"

The room was dark, save for a small puddle of moonlight on the well-worn rug. No lights were on. From deep in the house the sounds of conversation seeped into the room. Gabe raised an eyebrow.

"Oh, I leave the TV on sometimes," explained Sharon, with little conviction. "The house is so quiet otherwise."

Gabe shrugged and turned his attention back to the dolly. He traced his fingers over the intricate engraving on the top plank of wood.

"Really is beautiful work."

Gabe turned. His fingers skimmed Sharon's cheek as they had the wood a moment before. Her skin exploded into a deep crimson fire.

"It would be a shame not to see the finished piece," he said.

No, Sharon. He won't understand.

Sharon shook her head, fighting against the doubt. She could do it. She could show him, explain. Then he would understand.

"Five, maybe five minutes?" she whispered. "I just have to fasten it together."

Gabe nodded.

"I'll make myself busy then."

He glanced at the large trash can in the kitchen straining to hold its contents under the lid.

"That's a good place to start."

Sharon whispered her consent and watched him step into the kitchen. He moved with grace and confidence, a drastic contrast to the lumbering beast that had resided here so many months before. It seemed right.

You're wrong, Sharon. Oh, so wrong.

She set to work. She knew every inch of the piece, every knot and grain. In truth, this would be the first time even she would see it fully put together, though she had pictured it since its inception. Within minutes she had fixed the sides in place to the top and bottom edge—two long and two short at a 70-degree angle. The dowels slid in expertly. Only the lid remained. She set it flush with the sides, satisfied by the crisp suction of the tight fit, and attached the hinges. As she tightened the final screw, Gabe returned.

"Well, I don't think that smell is coming from the trash. Maybe a squirrel died in your attic or something."

He stopped at the edge of the carpet, his face betraying both confusion and alarm.

"Is that what I think it is?"

Sharon's face fell in shame.

He doesn't get it. He thinks you're a loser, too.

"It's kind of morbid, don't you think? I mean, a coffin?"

Sharon backed away, arms itching with embarrassment.

Fool. Such a fool!

"Is it symbolic?" asked Gabe.

Sharon couldn't speak. She faded deeper into the shadows of the hallway towards the back room. Gabe turned, now aware of his bungled reaction.

"No, I mean, it's just unexpected," he stammered. He followed her down the hall, stumbling over his words. "Sharon, I'm sorry. It just took me by surprise."

Sharon felt the world shrink around her. The darkness closed in a tight circle, narrowing her vision to a pinpoint as if she was looking through the wrong end of a telescope. She fell against the door of the back room and tumbled inside.

"Sharon? Are you okay?"

The room was spinning. Sharon braced herself against the rank moldy couch behind her, fingers slipping on the slick leather. She saw a miniature Gabe enter the room at the far end of her tunnel vision and she didn't have the strength to stop him.

Stay out! Don't see!

The stench in the room knocked Gabe's head back as if he had been hit in the face.

"Sharon?" he choked. "Good lord, what is that?"

Sharon crumbled to the floor.

No! Go away.

Gabe did not help her up, his attention was fixed on the mess of bones and cloth plastered to the cushions.

"Is that your *husband*?"

Gabe's words came out muffled. He was struggling to breathe, his mouth and nose shoved deep into his elbow. The body on the couch—Gabe could only assume it was a body—looked as if it had melted into the leather, merged with it. A pulsating heat radiated from it like a dying fire.

"Sharon, what did you do?"

Sharon didn't respond. She was slumped against the back of the couch, eyes open, but unfocused.

I'm sorry! This isn't what I wanted....

She watched the rest unfold in front of her as if she were seated in a private theater. She saw herself rise up, level with Gabe. He looked confused, maybe even frightened. Sharon felt her fingers wrap around something hard. From the corner of her eye it came into view. It looked familiar, maybe one of the baseball bats from *his* collection. She watched as it struck Gabe across his newly trimmed beard.

So sorry.

Gabe fell, his legs folding up underneath him. Another blow. Sharon couldn't watch anymore. She looked away. It would be better in the morning. In the background the TV rambled on. Somehow everything was always better in the morning.

DROUGHT

Another record-breaking day here in Athens this afternoon. High of 96, and still not a drop in sight. This extends the rainless streak to an even one hundred days. Water restrictions are still in effect, so nothing to do today but stay inside and watch it all wilt and die. Happy sweating, y'all.

Ed Towns switched off the radio and sank deeper into his La-Z-Boy. Outside his window the sun was just clearing the Chase Street Bridge, shards of light cutting gashes into his formerly award-winning lawn. Sixteen. That was the last count of dead spots. Sixteen, and that was just the front yard. Hours of hard work pissed away in the name of conservation.

"Global warming," Ed muttered with a somber chuckle. He swirled his breakfast bourbon around once more, studying his hands. They were once thick, callused tools. He traced the scar that cut like a river across his mountainous knuckles, following it around to his wrist where it grew to a fat worm-sized reminder of his impotence. He downed his drink. At the sound of the ice clinking against the side of the glass, Titus raised his head and gave two swift slaps of his tail. Ritual. Ed glanced over at the dog, who was half-on, half-off his bed. Two more slaps of that thick tail. Ed nodded. With a grunt, he hoisted himself up and ambled to the front door. Titus met him there, leash in mouth. Ed slipped the loop through his collar and opened the door. The wet heat slapped him in the face like a damp rolled-up towel. Beads of sweat formed immediately at the base of his neck and slithered down beneath his shirt. How could it be this humid and not rain? Ed contemplated going out to the yard and watering the lawn with his own sweat. Probably too salty, he thought.

Titus shook himself from head to tail and Ed snapped back to reality.

"Yeah, come on, boy."

They left the yard and went out through the side gate onto New Avenue. Up the hill, Titus glanced casually at the small terrier running back and forth just inside the chain-link fence, yapping furiously.

"Shut up, ya mutt," said Ed. He watched as the small dog leaped up against a low wall and took a bite at Titus through the fence. Titus loomed over the terrier, unconcerned. Ed considered kicking the little snot off the wall, but decided to save his energy. It was too hot. Instead he called to the house.

"Matthews!"

No answer, but Ed could see movement behind the window shades. The terrier continued barking. Titus pulled on the leash, eager to move on, or perhaps just impatient with this part of the ritual.

"Keep an eye on your dog, Matthews, or I will!" Ed yelled at the house. He kicked the bottom of the fence and the terrier jumped back, yelping as it slunk back up toward the house, where Matthews' skinny arm appeared to hold the screen door open so it could scurry back inside.

"Loser," Ed chuckled to himself, pleased. He had developed quite a mean streak in the years since Patty had left him.

Titus pulled harder on the leash and they moved on into the sunlight of Nacoochee. The rancid smell of the nearby chicken processing plant followed them down the hill toward the train tracks. They rarely took this route, but today Ed reveled in the desiccated yards and shriveled gardens they passed. Maybe his sixteen dead spots weren't so bad. A block later, turning onto Chattooga, Ed stopped. Two houses down on the left, across from the water tower, a fig tree grew, taut and defiant, with thick, full leaves. Most of the yard was brown, but there was a wide circle of green grass surrounding the tree trunk that spread out in tendrils, creating a lush pinwheel effect.

"Goddamn," Ed muttered. His brown lawn flashed through his mind, mocking him.

He and Titus approached the tree, hesitant, like explorers happening upon some lost sacred ground. Ed glanced up at the house. It was a well-maintained Craftsman-style bungalow, single story with a large front porch. It was in good shape—fresh paint, new gutters. Someone had fixed it up. Ed stepped onto the spongy turf underneath the tree and it cradled his shoe like a thick bath mat, giving Ed the insane urge to remove his shoes and scrunch his toes into the rich soil underneath.

"Hiya," said a voice from the porch. On instinct, Ed drew his foot back off the grass.

"Hot one today, isn't it?" continued the voice. Ed looked up to see a slim man in his forties glide down off the porch. He was barefoot, wearing a tight-fitting polo shirt with his pants rolled up past his ankles. The pants looked expensive. The feet looked tan and soft. This was not a man who worked hard for a living.

Ed nodded and shook the man's hand as he bounded up to him. More soft tan skin.

"Leonard," said the man. "Leonard Yorst."

"Ed."

The man waited, and then shrugged as Ed did not offer his last name. He bent down to Titus and rubbed him behind the ears with both hands.

"And who might this little guy be?" Leonard asked. He jostled Titus' large head back and forth. Titus didn't seem to mind.

"Titus," answered Ed.

"No last name either, eh, Titus?" Leonard asked, scrunching his nose up against Titus' sloppy nostrils. "Ah well, we can't have everything, can we, little guy?"

Ed tugged on the leash and Titus sat down. Off the grass.

"You could lose your hand next time, petting a dog like that without asking."

"Well," continued Leonard, ignoring the thinly veiled threat. "Y'all in the mood for coffee?"

Ed cringed. He had said *y'all* as if reading it from a book, exaggerated and unfamiliar. Definitely not from Georgia.

"Just admiring your tree," said Ed.

"Oh, yeah. It's coming along. It's a lot of work to keep it growing, but I was like, 'I can't allow myself to quit,' you know? Would seem a bit sacrilegious on my part."

He winked and patted Ed on the shoulder.

"Why? You an expert of some sort?"

Leonard took a step back and gave a theatrical bow.

"Dr. Leonard Yorst, botanist. I work over at the university, specializing in plant/insect interplay. Pollination, agriculture stuff. Lots of fun."

Figures, thought Ed.

"They know about the water restrictions over there?"

Leonard laughed.

"Of course we do, Ed. We're the ones who help determine the rationing."

"It's against the law to water outside."

"Technically, it's an ordinance."

"Still ain't right. Someone might call the cops."

Leonard raised an eyebrow.

"Interesting observation."

Leonard squared his shoulders and raised two fingers on his right hand.

"Scout's honor, Sir. I am not using city water on my tree or yard."

Two fingers, thought Ed. Didn't even make it past Cub Scouts. Ed eyed the tree and then the grass. Leonard followed his gaze.

"No offense, Ed, but I don't see you as much of a science guy," said Leonard. "Am I wrong?"

Ed didn't respond.

"Well, there's more than one way to feed your garden," continued Leonard. "Or skin a cat, you might say. I'm an experimental botanist, Ed, which means I look for new ways—sometimes even revisit old ways—of maximizing outcomes. In fact, this tree is the result of a new technique I've been working on. I can see you're intrigued by my success."

Ed nodded reluctantly.

"Well," said Leonard. He wrapped a conspiratorial arm around the bigger man's shoulders. "A magician never reveals his secrets, now, does he, Ed?"

With a wide smile, Leonard brushed a yellowjacket off Ed's sleeve.

"But, I never like to leave my audience disappointed," continued Leonard. "So, here's a fun fact for you, Ed No-Last-Name. Did you know the yellowjacket is a meat eater? Yep. So much so that it's other name is the 'meat bee', though as you know, it's not a bee at all. As such, they eat most everything that goes along with meat: blood, tissue, fat. The workers 'process' it into a thick liquid and feed it to the young. Pretty remarkable."

Leonard hopped back and produced another exaggerated bow.

"Anyhoo, if it's still a 'no' on that coffee then, Ed?"

Without waiting for a response, or permission, Leonard leaned down and tousled the thick fur behind Titus' ears one more time.

"Y'all take care now, okay?"

Ed winced again. He watched Leonard Yorst's bare feet dance across the grass, nimbly avoiding the driest patches, and disappear around the house. His eyes burned. What a pretentious turd, talking to him like a child. All the while Ed could see he was lying; see it in his smug eyes, in the taunting richness of the grass, in the damn fig tree. Ed churned up a healthy—or, rather, unhealthy—glob of snot and phlegm and launched it at the tree. He glanced at Titus.

"Come on, boy," he said under his breath. He shoved the dog forward with his knee. "Here's a good spot."

Titus wouldn't budge. Ed kneed him again.

"Do it, Titus."

No movement. Ed shook his head in disgust.

"Stupid dog. I'll do it then."

He walked over to the tree, behind it, out of view of the house. He could feel the bourbon still swirling around in his stomach, and figured some must have made it through by now. He unzipped his pants, but hesitated. He glanced at the house. Screw it. He could handle that little jerk if he came back. Still, he kept one eye on the house until he was done, making sure to get plenty on the grass too.

"Welcome to the neighborhood," he grunted. With a sharp tug on the leash, he led Titus back onto the road.

That evening Ed replayed the scene over and over in his head. Where did that guy get off? A fancy degree didn't give him the right to cheat everyone else out of water. Ed slumped down into his chair and refilled his glass. From the kitchen he could hear Titus lap up the rest of his daily ration. Ed took a long sip. He would go back when it was dark; that's when a coward like Leonard Yorst would try and water that tree. He finished his drink and poured another. Yeah, that's what he would do.

Ed peered out through the tall bamboo on the crest of the hill above the train tracks. He had chosen his position wisely. It was difficult to hear clearly due to the constant nearby buzzing that Ed attributed to the low-hanging power lines, but his line of sight was clear. He had a great view of the side yard and the fig tree, but was also concealed in part by the steel legs of the water tower on his left. He didn't have to wait long. Soon after 11:00, a thin shadow darted down the porch stairs and around the side of the house. *Scout's honor!* thought Ed, and snorted. The shadow flitted back to the front yard toward the tree. Ed could not see a hose, but Yorst was clearly carrying something. His shadow slipped past the fig tree and started across the road, straight toward Ed.

Ed squeezed back into the bamboo, but there was nowhere to go. Leonard's shadow reached the side of the road and stopped under the water tower. He was swinging a bucket and whistling a low tune. Ed leaned forward, curious in spite of himself. Leonard reached up and pulled a rope, lowering a thin ladder that connected to the rusty one on the water tower itself. With agile ease, Leonard climbed up and out of sight, whistling the whole way.

"Son of a bitch!" said Ed out loud. Over the tinny buzz, he could hear Leonard banging around up inside the tower. It had been unused and presumably empty for as long as Ed could remember, so it hadn't even crossed his mind that the tower was where Yorst was getting his water. Something whizzed by his ear, and Ed swatted it away.

He crept up to the tower and behind the ladder. Craning his neck, Ed could see the outline of a trap door. It was thin rusted metal and Leonard hadn't closed it completely. A steady drip of liquid was pooling on the top rung and now dribbled down the rail. Ed rolled a bit around in his fingers. It had a strange viscosity to it, like motor oil, and it was tacky. Ed held his fingers up to the moonlight to examine them and something landed on his thumb. Instinctually, he smashed it into his palm. A pinprick of pain shot through his hand. Ed flipped his hand over. Crushed up amongst the liquid was a yellowjacket. The stinger had gone into his palm, just above his scar.

What the hell was a yellowjacket doing out here at night?

Ed flung the insect to the ground just as Leonard came sliding down the ladder, almost on top of him. Ed stumbled backward, banging his head on the tower leg. Leonard wheeled around at the noise, sloshing some of the contents of the bucket onto the ground. Ed moved forward, shaking his head to help clear it. Regaining his composure, he squared up to Leonard, making himself as large as possible.

"I knew you were a liar," Ed said. "Knew it the moment I saw you."

Leonard took a step back. His eyes were wide, but not in surprise. They seemed almost curious.

"Are you going to call the police?" he asked in a conversational tone.

"I should," said Ed.

Leonard cocked his head to the side at the hesitation.

"But you won't," he said. It wasn't quite a question.

"I want to know what's in the bucket. It ain't water. That tower's been dry for years."

"Interesting observation," said Leonard. He jiggled the handle of the bucket, slopping more liquid onto the ground. "Remember our little science lesson from earlier, Ed? You don't want to know what's in here. I don't think you'd understand. Like I said, I don't think you and science mix all that well."

Ed moved closer. He stood at least a head taller and outweighed Leonard by more than fifty pounds, yet when he reached out his hand it was trembling.

"Let me see."

Leonard shrugged and lifted the bucket up. He held it in front of him for a second, then tilted it, letting the contents pour out. A thin syrup spewed on to the ground. Even in the moonlight Ed could tell it was too dark and chunky to be water. He watched it pool at his feet, overflowing a small divot in the dirt. Something solid toppled into the small puddle with a splash. It floated to the surface and Ed could make out an object pale in color and about three inches long. Ed looked up to see Leonard staring at him, a tight smile betraying his amusement.

"Oops!" said Leonard.

In an instant he was beside Ed, twisting his arm up high behind his back. Ed heard a sharp crack, like a dry stick snapping under a heavy boot, and his arm fell limp. Pain shot out from his shoulder in all directions, but his scream was cut short by a sharp blow from Leonard's elbow. Ed crashed to the ground, face-first into the pool. He tasted salt, and metal. Blood, he thought. Too much, though. Something was wrong. He turned to spit, but his jaw flopped to the side and the blood oozed down his cheek. Broken. He felt Leonard's fingers thread through his hair and pull his head out of the puddle. Before being slammed back to the ground, Ed identified the object in the blood. It was a finger.

Hours later, Ed stirred awake. He was propped up under the fig tree. He was freezing.

"Do you know anything about the fig wasp, Ed?"

He tried to push himself up, but he couldn't get his hands to work, couldn't even really feel them at all. Leonard nudged him with his bare foot.

"Fun fact. The fig, though absolutely tasty, is rather disgusting."

Leonard had on a tight white undershirt, sweaty and stained with dirt. He was hovering over Ed, leaning on the end of a shovel.

"Yep, fascinating, but disgusting. The female wasp burrows into the fig and lays its eggs. If the fig is male, the eggs hatch. Inside the fig."

Leonard leaned down close to Ed's cheek. Whispering.

"Don't worry. We don't actually eat the male figs."

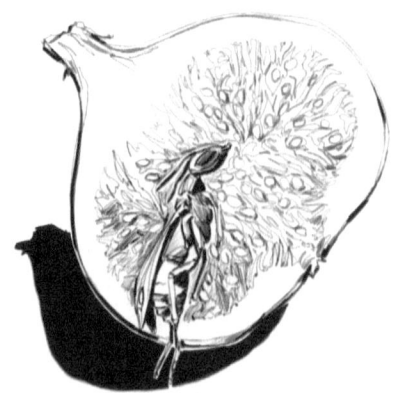

He patted Ed on the cheek causing his loose jaw to swing side to side in excruciating pain.

"No, we eat the female ones, Ed. See, the entry hole is so small that when the wasp crawls in, it loses its wings, often even the antennae, gets trapped, and dies. But, it's not in vain. The fig feeds on the wasp and makes the fruit."

Ed was shivering. Why was he so cold?

"You're going to be my wasp, Ed."

Leonard brushed the matted hair back from Ed's eyes and gently steadied his head against a branch. Ed could see rivulets of blood inching their way into the dry grass. His blood. It was spurting out from all over, running down his chest, from under his legs, everywhere. Ed shook uncontrollably. So cold.

"So, that new technique you were so curious about," Leonard continued, standing over him, silhouetted against the moon. "It certainly seems to be working."

Leonard peered up at the tree and plucked off a yellowjacket that had perched there. He watched it flit around his palm.

"Wasps truly are amazing," he said. "So industrious, so versatile, so useful."

He glanced down at Ed's ashen body. Ed was having trouble holding his eyes open; they were too heavy. So tired. Leonard set the shovel against a branch and knelt down. He placed the yellowjacket just above Ed's abdomen. Ed watched in horror as the wasp dipped its head into a streak of blood and started drinking.

"And to think, Ed. All this is only a third of what I'll get out of you."

Leonard then grabbed Ed's hands as if getting ready to drag him across the yard. Ed saw this happening, but felt nothing. His hands and arms were completely numb up to the shoulder.

"I'm going to put you in the water tower with the colony," said Leonard. "But you're a rather large man, and while that's great news for my yellowjackets, unfortunately, it means you won't quite fit in the hole. Needless to say, I've made some adjustments, just like our friend the fig wasp."

With that, Leonard snatched up Ed's arms, lifting them to eye-level. They had been severed at the shoulder. Ed felt nothing, he was too weak. Probably drugged. He watched as Leonard tossed his arms one by one into a shallow pit. Ed's eyes closed.

"I'll be back when you're all dried out. Can't exactly leave you out here on the front lawn, can I?"

Ed opened his eyes again to see Leonard walking, almost skipping, up the porch steps. Dozens of yellowjackets were gathered around his arm stumps, several more buzzed around his chest. A frail breeze drifted past, bringing a fetor of decay with it. *Always thought that smell came from the chicken plant*, was Ed's final thought before he shut his eyes for good.

DUSK

Boulevard Woods, the new little city park that had until recently been a forgotten, overgrown lot, was teeming with life in the early evening heat. Sweaty kids raced around the circular yard in plastic foot-pedaled cars. Just beyond the knee-high stone wall, a woman was busy picking cotton candy out of her son's hair, desperate to turn it into a teaching moment: *See, Travis, that's why we sit still while we eat, not try to somersault over our food.* A group of seven-year-olds emerged from the trailhead, arms filled with pinecones, their shirts and shorts stained with the sap they had wiped off on them. They sat down and began dividing up their treasure. In the middle of the park stood a tiny redhead in a bright blue dress. Her skin was covered in temporary tattoos from her gift bag and she was standing with her legs wide, arms lifted to the sky like a warrior princess. It was a happy bedlam.

Megan Cook watched all of this with pride. She was perched above on the sidewalk, enjoying the success of her endeavor: The First Annual Boulevard Woods Day in the Park. Two years of tumultuous committee meetings, political posturing, and bureaucratic prostitution had paid off. She had won. The turnout for the event was great, even higher than she had expected. What was unfolding in front of her was exactly what she had envisioned: a safe, enjoyable outdoor space for kids and families.

"You're all in danger!" someone yelled from the edge of the park. Megan turned—as did everyone within earshot—to see who it was.

"Danger!" the voice repeated.

It was Lance Weathers. Lance Weathers was 87 years old, born and raised in Boulevard and the last original resident of the area. The decades had not been kind to him. Widowed and childless, he had decided to take out his frustration on Boulevard Woods.

He had petitioned the county commissioners, interrupted town hall meetings with his incoherent ramblings, and even circulated pamphlets warning of the perils of the park. He reminded Megan of her grandfather when the dementia had set in, but before it had claimed his entire mind.

By the time Megan got closer, two fathers in their early thirties had blocked Lance from where the children were and ushered him back toward the street. While they seemed gentle enough, Megan could see their bodies tense with each of Lance's continual shouts.

"You're scaring the kids, sir," said one of the fathers.

"They should be scared!" replied Lance, with a snarl. Then louder, to the people in the park.

"You should all be scared!"

"Sir," said the other father. "You need to leave. Now."

Lance's pupils were dilated and his eyes scanned frantically from left to right. His sagging wrinkled jowls gave him the look of a sad basset hound, but there was legitimate fear in his eyes.

Megan stepped in.

"Mr. Weathers, there's no reason to do this."

Lance stared past them, fixing his eyes on the group of seven-year-olds and their pinecones.

"Get out!" he yelled. "Get away from there!"

Lance was frantic now, straining against Father Number Two. His lips peeled back, revealing stained broken teeth.

"It comes from the woods!"

Megan moved closer, placing a hand on his arm. It was damp with sweat.

"Mr. Weathers, please. This is not the time."

A crowd had formed along the edge of the grass, parents trying to both protect their children and get a better glimpse at the scene. Most of the children were oblivious, still running around in a melee, but a few of the older ones had gathered closer to their parents, concerned.

"Mr. Weathers," continued Megan. She realized she was now stroking his arm as one would a frightened dog. "Lance!"

She said this more forcefully than intended, but it had the desired effect. Lance snapped out of his fury. His eyes seemed to clear, to refocus. He looked at Megan with confusion.

"Miss Cook?"

"Mr. Weathers. Let me walk you home."

Lance managed a weak nod. Megan glanced at Father Number Two and he released the old man's arm, if reluctantly. Searching the crowd, Megan saw Michael and nodded. He would know what to do. Indeed, before she and Lance were even in the street, she could hear Michael's rich baritone voice drift through the park, attempting to calm everyone down.

Lance Weathers lived just down the hill on Barber Street, close enough to hear the festivities in the park, but at the wrong angle to see anything.

"Mr. Weathers," Megan said, guiding him up his porch steps, "You know what the commission said. Another outburst and someone's going to get a restraining order against you. They're kids, Mr. Weathers. They're just having fun. You can't be scaring them like that."

"Kids...." Lance muttered. He unlocked the rusty deadbolt and pried his front door open. He paused, hand on the door as if it was holding him and not the other way around.

"You went too far," he said.

Megan took a step back.

"What?" she asked.

Lance shook his head.

"Too far. That's *its* home and now you've gone and opened it up to the public. That park is not safe." He narrowed his eyes at her. "And neither are you."

Megan backed down off the porch. She half expected him to leap out at her.

"What do you mean?"

Lance smiled. A sad pained smile.

"You'll see."

He shut the door. Megan heard deadbolts locking, heard him move away, but no lights were turned on. He simply shuffled into the darkness.

"Good grief!" she said aloud, unsure if it was his intermittent lucidity that troubled her, or what had come out of his mouth during those moments.

When Megan got back to the park, the crowd had thinned to a maybe a dozen people. She heard mumblings of *wolf* from the few who remained. Michael was rounding up the stray plastic cars.

"I tried to keep them here," said Michael. "But everyone just kept eyeing the trail and whispering. Eventually one family left, and then another, like they were tethered to each other."

Megan sighed. She walked down to the trailhead, with Michael a step behind.

"What do you think?" she asked.

"You know the story. We all do."

"Yeah, but come on. No way there's a wolf running around in the middle of town."

Michael shrugged. Megan glanced over toward Barber Street. She could just make out the rusted roof of Lance's house.

"The Wolf of Boulevard," Megan continued. "My grandfather would tell me all sorts of stories about it. Dead squirrels, mangled pets; he even said it killed a 'hobo' back when he was in high school."

"Hobo?"

"Yeah, well, that's how he put it."

Michael chuckled.

"How about you?" asked Megan.

"College." Michael shrugged. "The stories just kind of circulated around. Kids would come down here and try to find it. Take a picture of it or something, like Bigfoot. Really just another place to get drunk."

Megan peered down the trail. It was so tranquil, so peaceful. So perfect.

"I called Animal Control," said Michael, interrupting the silence. "They can meet one of us here late, after they finish their 'priority' calls."

"One of us?"

"I presumed you would want to be the one, but didn't want to assume."

Megan smiled. He was good.

"Yes, I do."

"Besides," Michael said. "I've got plans. You know it's Friday, right?"

"Once upon a time I did."

Megan sighed again. "You go on, Michael. I'll finish up and wait for Animal Control."

"You sure?"

"You're the one with the plans tonight."

"True. Thanks."

With that he was gone. Megan stood alone for a moment. That was what she was, alone, like Lance Weathers. This park was all she had right now. It was her baby. She grabbed a few forgotten toys off the path and set them by the front sign. There would be more down the trail, and tidying up gave her something to do while she waited for Animal Control.

A while later Megan made her way back toward the park, arms laden with so many toys she wondered if they had been dropped by the children or tossed out by the parents. The sun had long set and the woods were quiet. A piercing, isolated screech of what might have been a barred owl broke the silence and was gone. As Megan crested the hill at the trailhead it was full dark and difficult to see, but in the weak glow of the streetlight she could make out a figure just below the stone wall. Its head was down, staring at the ground as it walked. *Animal Control*, she thought. The figure moved into the shadow of the wall.

"Hi," Megan said, moving forward. "Find some tracks?"

The figure didn't turn around. He, at least it looked like a he, moved away from the park, toward the woods. His hand was out, tracing along the wall as if feeling for something, but as he stepped into a pool of light from the streetlight, Megan could see there was something wrong about the way he moved. She thought it had been someone from Animal Control looking for signs, but the figure was shuffling his feet, not tracing the wall, but leaning on it for support. He was hurt.

"Sir?" she said. She dropped the toys and moved toward him. The man lurched forward.

"Get back," he mumbled. He hunched over and vomited on the ground. "I don't know where it went."

Megan went rigid. She knew that voice.

"Lance?" she whispered.

The man didn't answer. He vomited again and fell to his knees. Against her will Megan moved closer, kneeling down next to him. It was Lance, and he was seriously injured. One arm hung loose at the shoulder and the other clutched at his stomach, which was spilling his insides all over the ground. He spit onto the ground. It wasn't vomit; it was blood. More words gurgled out of his mouth, wet and pained.

"What?" Megan asked. She couldn't stand to look at him. She lowered her ear to hear him speak, but kept her eyes averted.

"Wolf...." Lance whispered.

Megan didn't hear this; her full attention was on the two quarter-sized red circles staring at her from the edge of the park. She shrank back as the creature emerged. It was grotesque, a hideous combination of human and animal. Hairless limbs with long-taloned fingers shot out beneath tufts of thick-furred paws. Fangs protruded from its snoutless face, like a poorly made Halloween mask. It moved on all fours, but awkwardly, as if unsure how to make all of his limbs work together.

Megan felt something clutch at her arm. It was Lance. She had crawled up on top of him, smothering him. She scuttled off to the side and the creature snarled. She felt it size her up in an effort to determine how much of a threat she was. Megan's mind was in turmoil; she couldn't think straight. *Don't run*, she thought, remembering what people always said about bears. Even as she said it, she felt her feet turn. The creature's attention was drawn to her movement. It snarled again and rose up on its hind legs.

Something whizzed by Megan's ear and struck the creature in the shoulder. Megan turned and ran, forgetting about the stone wall. With a crash, she crumpled to the ground. Something struck the wolf again, this time just below the eye. It moved more comfortably now on two legs, pivoting back toward Lance.

"Play dead!" Lance gasped.

"Lance, no!" Megan groaned. Her nose was bleeding, the blood running down into her mouth.

"Play dead!" Lance coughed. More blood. "I told you. You're in danger."

He looked at Megan and their eyes met. He was lucid. He had always been lucid, Megan realized. Lance drew back his arm to throw another rock and the creature lunged. Megan saw the creature wince, but it kept going. It leaped over Megan and engulfed Lance. The two of them rolled away toward the center of the park. Megan heard something snap and then what sounded like a watermelon splattering on a sidewalk. Then quiet. *Play dead*, she thought. She closed her eyes and curled up against the wall. Somewhere behind her the creature moved. Circling her. *Play dead*. The wolf drew closer. She could smell a mix of urine and blood. Was it hers? Hot breath on her neck. She felt talons dig into her shoulder as a hand shook her once. Twice. *Play dead*. And she did.

She played dead while the creature ate what was left of Lance. She played dead while it dragged the remains out of the park. She played dead until she passed out from exhaustion.

A trio of runners found Megan early the next morning. She was mumbling incoherently about a wolf. Physical examination revealed that she had suffered a mild concussion and a broken nose. Her psychiatric evaluation, though, was less enthusiastic. Following weeks of psychotropic meds and therapy, the conclusions seemed obvious: post-traumatic stress disorder; severe paranoia with hallucinations; and possible schizophrenia.

There was no corroborating her story, no body, no signs of a struggle, and certainly no wolf.

Whatever had become of Lance Weathers, he had disappeared without a trace.

Weeks later, after it was agreed that, Miss Cook's unfortunate fate aside, Boulevard Woods would be officially reopened, Michael gazed down at the bustling park. Everything was humming along fine. Kids raced around, chasing each other in a game of tag, parents chatted in groups around the periphery, and the air was filled with the enticing aroma of the nearby food carts—Michael's new addition.

"Sir?" came a voice from behind him. Michael turned.

"Yes?"

"Thirteen."

"How many?

"Thirteen, sir. We found them scattered up and down the path. Even some near the road."

"All right, thanks."

Michael shook his head. Something was killing the squirrels in and around the park. He looked up to the trees. *Owls?* He thought. Maybe he would come back tonight to check it out.

Dusk

OLD PAL

The light turned green on Prince Avenue and an old Ford pickup truck ambled off down the street towards downtown. It was early afternoon on a Saturday in Athens, but there was an away game this week so traffic was quiet. The whole town was dead. Carlos Sanchez and Ben Hibble hadn't been able to get tickets to the game, so they were collectively stewing in their own misfortune over a late lunch at Automatic Pizza. Their friends were living it up in Tuscaloosa and they were stuck here in a ghost town with nothing to do. They needed something, some sort of adventure, or at the least a good story to spit back in the faces of their friends who were undoubtedly going to have some of their own when they got back. After a few beers, the conversation had turned to urban legends.

"You heard the one about the rabid wolf in Boulevard Woods?" asked Ben. "We could check that out."

Carlos turned back to the table and shoved the last bite of pizza into his mouth. He swallowed it without chewing and washed it down with the last of his beer; he liked to time his meals perfectly. He belched and rolled his eyes.

"Whatever," Carlos said. "Everybody knows that's a hoax. I heard it was part of Alpha Phi's hazing."

"Anything else, boys?"

Ben jumped a little as the waiter reached past him to clear his plate. He had a solid band tattoo just above his elbow and the word *Beyond* written vertically from elbow to wrist. Carlos pegged him immediately for a local.

"Yeah, actually," said Carlos. He crumpled his napkin and tossed it on the table where his plate had been. "We've been discussing urban legends."

The waiter eyed the napkin, then slowly swept it off the table. He looked over at Carlos.

"Look," continued Carlos. "I know you've heard us talking. Hell, you've been out here to clean these tables three times and we're the only people here. So I know you're interested. I just want to know if you've got anything to contribute, or if you just like to watch."

Carlos leaned back and spread his arms out wide, palms open, both an invitation and a challenge. The waiter reached across the table again and took the empty beer glass, dropping the napkin inside before he placed it on the tray.

"Yeah," he replied. "I know one. Might be just right for a couple of *boys* like you."

He paused for effect and glanced over at Ben, pursing his lips but stopping short of making the accompanying kissing sound. Ben blushed in spite of himself.

"We're not, like, together," Ben said too quickly.

"Relax, Ben," said Carlos. He was smiling. He liked the attitude on this waiter. "He's just messing with you."

The waiter leaned in towards Ben. A sickly sweet smell drifted out of the waiter's collar that reminded Ben of rotting spinach. Ben leaned back, but there was nowhere to go without standing up, so he just stared at the floor, trying to maintain control. The waiter flashed a cigarette-yellowed smile and took Ben's plate. He nodded across the street.

"Why not start there?"

Hands deep in the pockets of his Old Navy khakis, Carlos glanced over at the brown and white sign hanging above the Old Pal across Prince Avenue. It promised Bar and Cocktails, nothing more. Simple.

"'The Old Pal'?" asked Carlos.

"Yeah," the waiter said. "Group of old guys gathers there once a month, during the full moon, if you believe one version."

"So?"

"So, they make a specialty drink. They call it a 'Stiff One.' Supposedly it tastes like piss, but pumps you up like you're on steroids. Some say after you drink it you can see in the dark."

Ben leaned back from the table to get a better look. He scratched idly at his cheek. His beard was at a middle stage where it itched constantly, established but still somewhere short of true hipster length.

"So, what's the story?" he asked.

The waiter set their plates on a nearby table and wiped his hands. He sat down across from Carlos, placing his elbows on the table, and settled in to the tale, lowering his voice even though the patio was empty and no one was around to hear.

"Once a month, the Old Pal gets a limited shipment of an Irish liquor, dark red and bitter as hell. They mix it with some kind of local, home-brewed hooch and serve it warm and neat, with a rare Algerian white olive. The sick thing is, the liquor soaks into these tiny veins in the olive and turns them red, too, so it looks like an eye. Supposed to signify drinking the blood of your enemy."

"Nice," said Carlos. "That's got promise. Who are the old guys?"

"They call themselves the 'Inner Circle.' They're a cult, the only ones who know how to make the drink. They do it in the middle of the day so no one's likely to come in and mess up their ritual. Legend has it they take blood from the newest member and add it to the mix, as a pledge of devotion."

"What? I ain't doing that!" said Ben, flinching as if the waiter were threatening to take that pledge of devotion from him right there. The waiter winked at him.

"Don't worry, little one," he said, patting Ben on the knee. "That's only if you want to join the cult. For your...experiment... all you have to do is get in and try the drink.

"Now, that's much easier," the waiter continued. "You go in and have a look around, but don't be obvious about it. Act like you know what you're doing, like you belong there. If you notice anyone gathered in a group, walk out; they're still in the middle of the ritual."

He leaned in, serious now, trying to bring home the gravity of the scenario. "You got it? Don't mess with the ritual."

Ben and Carlos nodded. The waiter leaned back and smiled his yellowed smile.

"If everything looks cool, go straight up to the bar. Tell the bartender you want a 'stiff one' and that Ray sent you, that you're an 'old pal' of his. Simple."

Yeah, thought Carlos. Simple, like the sign.

"One more thing," said the waiter as he gathered up the plates. "Go in one at a time."

"Why?" asked Ben.

"The last thing you want to do is draw attention to yourselves. So, space it out. One of you go in first," he paused and pointed at Carlos. "I'd suggest *you,* since this one's way too skittish."

Ben blushed again. The waiter shrugged.

"Just a suggestion. Take it or leave it." He wiped the table once more and went inside.

Carlos turned to Ben, who was still staring across the street. He clapped his hands together in triumph. Ben jumped.

"Perfect," said Carlos. "This is perfect!"

Ben shook his head. This sounded way worse than anything else they had come up with.

"Seriously," said Carlos. "This has everything we need. Nobody from campus comes down here, so it's this mysterious Normaltown bar. It's got a cult, a secret drink, blood. It's perfect!"

Carlos moved around the table and put an arm around Ben's shoulders like a coach getting his quarterback ready to lead a final comeback drive. "Come on. Look, I'll go first, like he said. Give me like ten minutes, then come in. If they ignore me, I'll come back out. But, if it works, you come in and try it too. The story will be better if we both do it."

Ben scratched his beard again and glanced up at the sky. Despite the early hour, the moon was there, just visible behind a thin layer of gray mist. It was indeed full. He took a deep breath and held it a moment.

"All right, let's do it," he exhaled.

Carlos slapped him on the back. "There you go!"

They crossed Prince Avenue and Ben took up position outside the P&M Army store. After a long ten minutes of reading and rereading the handmade postings on the store windows, he went into the Old Pal.

The room was not exactly bright, but it lacked the intimidating dimness of a daytime bar that offered as many pools of darkness and shadowy corners as it did patrons. Yet, at the same time, Ben had the sensation of looking into a sunlit lake that allowed you to see a foot or so deep, but cut off all light

41

below, the sensation that something was lurking beneath the surface, waiting for him to dip his feet in the water.

A handful of men was scattered about the tables, but there was no one at the bar. More importantly, no one was gathered in any sort of group. The ritual was over. There was no Carlos though, either. Maybe he was in the men's room or had slipped out another entrance to give Ben some space to act on his own.

Act like you know what you're doing, Ben told himself. He walked up to the bar, feeling all eyes in the room on him.

"Uh, Ray sent me," he stammered. The bartender made no move toward him, just continued to dry the highball glass in his hand. "I'm an old pal," he said, almost in a whisper.

"You sure?" asked the bartender. Ben managed to muster up a nod in response. He heard chairs scrape the wood floor as the others got to their feet. He felt the men gather around behind him. The bartender produced an opaque bottle from under the bar and placed it in front of Ben.

"Uncork it," he said. Ben fumbled with the top, but snapped the latch back. A sharp metallic odor snaked out of the bottle.

"Pour," said the bartender. He placed the highball glass down on the bar. Hands shaking, Ben poured the viscous red liquor into the glass until the bartender nodded. One of the other men reached around and topped off the glass with a clear liquid from his own flask.

The bartender set a large, thick-glassed container on the bar. It was filled with white olives floating in a thick syrupy liquid. Ben's stomach turned over. The bartender reached in and plucked one out, dropping it into the glass.

"Drink," he said.

Ben drank. The liquid was warm, more than room temperature, and sour. It burned as it slid down his throat, threatening to close it up. Ben gagged it down, but was left with the olive to contend with. He bit down. There was no pop, none of the discernible crispness that Ben associated with olives. Instead it felt like biting into a soft-boiled egg that hadn't quite cooked all the way through and was now leaking its innards into his mouth. He forced this all down and set the glass on the bar, closing his eyes.

When Ben opened his eyes, the room was spinning. He had to reach out and grab the bar to steady himself. He saw the bartender flash by, followed by the other men, as if he were standing in the center of a fairground whirl-a-wheel. The men were all smiling, pale lips giving way to sharp red-stained teeth. *Did he hear laughter?* He struggled to maintain control of his mind, make sense of what was happening around him. The stool gave way beneath him. He heard it shatter, but watched as it seemed to melt into the floor. *Wood couldn't melt, could it?* Ben saw but did not feel his head crash down against the bar, and he was sent reeling to the floor.

Ben was numb. He could feel the drink flow through his veins, removing all feeling from each part of his body—his hands, legs, ankles, and finally his feet. He was still conscious, but unable to move. The men who had gathered around him now parted, making way for the bartender. In his hand was a small paring knife.

"Thanks for the donation," he said, his lips curled back into a sick smile. "It's been a while since we had any walk-ins."

The hollow clink of the old brass door bell rang behind them. The bartender looked up.

"Want to do the honors, Ray?" he asked.

Ben heard footsteps on the wooden floor. The odor of rotten spinach drifted down to his nose and an arm reached out over him, grabbing the paring knife. Ben watched the tattooed letters appear one-by-one: D-N-O-Y-E-B. He looked up to find the puckered lips of the waiter from Automatic Pizza. This time he did make the kissing noise.

"Nothing personal, sweetie," he said, yellowed smile in full bloom. "This town just gets so boring sometimes."

A chuckle rippled through the group. Through the bartender's legs Ben could see a crumpled body in the corner. It was Carlos. He was missing an eye.

RUNNER'S HIGH

Garrison Shultz did not care for runners. Never had. The way they bounced in place on street corners in their expensive neon shoes, stunk up the early morning coffee shops, and dripped their pretentious sweat all over his car while they stretched in the parking lot offended him on a visceral level. No, he had never liked runners. His former boss Craig Lareby was a runner. For thirty-six years, Garrison had worked in the maintenance division at the university, probably since before that smug Lareby had even stopped pissing his diapers. Yet it had been Lareby—still in his damned Under Armour running shorts that showed way too much of his pasty thighs, his sweaty hands mucking up Garrison's desk calendar—who had let him go, sent him out to pasture with the rest of the useless junk that didn't fit in with today's "best practices" and "productivity objectives."

Garrison had taken it hard, packed everything he was allowed to take with him into a single cardboard box, gone home and started drinking. And drinking. The drinking led him to a well of deep, unresolved anger. The anger had opened some old wounds, deep-seated prejudices that dwelt in the repressed darkness of his soul. It was somewhere in that darkness where he crossed a line and Garrison had no interest in going back or healing the wounds; he liked the pain. He wanted others to feel it, too. Others like Craig Lareby.

Garrison Shulz had spent the last three decades roaming the laboratories of the university and had made friends. No, not friends, exactly—he didn't care too much for academics either—but he had met *faces*. Faces with notebooks and formulas. Faces who liked to talk about what they did. A lot. One face stood out, Dr. Jessica Prim, associate professor in the Department of Psychology and Assistant Director of the Behavioral Neuropharmacology Laboratory. She was doing what she called "exciting work with euphoriants" and their effect on the emotional state of her subjects, and how one particular new drug, PN-144, was showing great progress not only in heightening euphoria, but also other emotions. While small doses of the drug, given at the right stage, could increase euphoria and treat depression, the same dose given at the wrong stage would have the reverse effect—changing anger to rage, depression to suicidal ideations, even euphoria to mania— creating such heightened states of emotion that the subjects lost all control over their ability to reason.

Granted, Dr. Prim was working with rats, but Garrison didn't see why her findings couldn't be applied to the larger rats that ran through the streets at 5:30 AM their Fitbits beeping a constant reminder that they were on pace.

Garrison had watched one day as Dr. Prim administered the dose of PN-144 to her subjects. Within minutes the rats became living versions of whatever emotion they were experiencing at the time—crushing depression, blind euphoria, vicious rage—to the point where some collapsed in the corner, heartbroken and dying, or attacked everything in their environment, even killing other subjects, or simply leapt around until their hearts gave out. Whatever the beginning, the end always resulted in death.

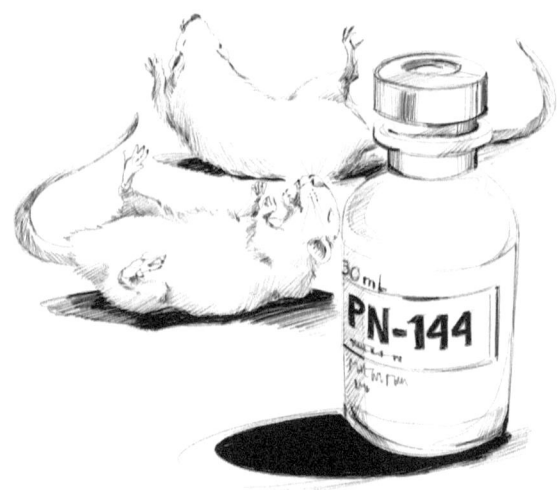

Garrison liked that idea.

"I still believe it's all a matter of titrating the dosing," Dr. Prim had explained. "I wouldn't dare suggest a clinical trial in humans at this point."

Pretending to listen, Garrison had smiled and thanked her and gone on his way, filing away this information for a later day. A day like today.

So, it was outside this lab where he found himself the morning after being fired. He had made his way through the back alleys and "maintenance only" corridors of the campus that he could have followed in his sleep, which was a good thing since his pounding hangover was making it hard to see straight. Garrison let himself into Dr. Prim's lab using one of the duplicated do-not-duplicate keys he kept on his personal key chain and replaced the vials of PN-144 with simple syrup - the rats would love that—and then made his way down to Sanford

Stadium. This was the staging area for the AthHalf, the annual half-marathon hosted by the city of Athens. He found the supply truck with the barrels for water station #1 and dumped in every drop of PN-144 he had, not even bothering to stir it.

At 7:42 AM, Garrison watched from his balcony on Hillcrest Avenue as the first runner went by. He was young and slim and hadn't broken a sweat; Garrison didn't think he had stopped for water. Too arrogant. At 7:54, a young blonde woman cut in front of an older man, almost tripping him up. The older man looked pissed, but didn't waste any breath shouting at her. Another runner glanced at his watch and frowned, probably not looking at a personal record today. *How disappointing*, Garrison thought dryly.

More and more runners went by, happy, sad, angry. The street became more congested as the mid-level runners passed through, slower. *Thirstier*, Garrison thought, and smiled.

He imagined the carnage to come, the bewilderment as police, campus authorities, and the media tried to figure out what had happened. It would be such a wonderful bedlam.

At 8:02 he heard the first screams from somewhere over on Milledge Avenue. Garrison wondered casually if the old man had taken revenge on that blonde for cutting him off. PN-144 was kicking in quickly, aided by the runners' increased blood flow. Garrison poured himself a cup of coffee, savoring the moment. With any luck, Craig Lareby would be passing by sometime soon. Maybe he would cut someone off, too. That would be a good show.

SCENES OF THE CRIMES
A WALK THROUGH THE BOULEVARD
NEIGHBORHOOD IN ATHENS, GEORGIA

ONETA WOODWORKS

Oneta Woodworks specializes in reclaimed millwork and repurposing old wood into new uses. In addition to Zack Brendel and his staff being some of the South's most skilled woodworkers, Oneta also produces highly individualized works thanks to their close working relationships with clients.

As of this printing, Oneta Woodworks does not offer any instructional classes. After this printing, they probably won't have any plans to do so either.

ATHENS WATER TOWERS

Perhaps the most recognizable water tower in Athens is located just over the bridge on Chase Street. It is host to a continual battle between local graffiti artists and county maintenance workers armed with buckets of brown paint.

The tower in this story is located next to the railroad tracks off a quiet side street and has long been forgotten. Or has it?

BOULEVARD WOODS

Still in its infancy, Boulevard Woods is a fresh new neighborhood park located at the corner of Boulevard and Barber Street. It sits on a 1.8-acre site, and features a short paved walking loop, an open lawn play area, and a quarter-mile trail. Boulevard Woods is not only designed for the neighborhood, but has largely been built by the neighborhood, with untold volunteer hours put in by individuals and local organizations.

The park is open daily from sunrise to sunset; however, it is highly recommended you leave the park by dusk.

AUTOMATIC PIZZA

From the moment the doors opened in 2015, Automatic Pizza has been a fixture in the Normaltown scene. Proprietor Bain Mattox transformed a defunct gas station into a quirky and stylish pizzeria that serves some of the best pizza in the area. Automatic also offers two outside dining areas: one overlooking Prince Ave. and the other tucked away on the back patio. Automatic was named winner of the 2017 Flagpole Magazine Reader Picks awards for Best Local Pizza.

At the time of this printing, there was nobody named Ray employed at Automatic.

THE OLD PAL

Since 2013, the Old Pal has anchored the north side of the Normaltown neighborhood. Owners Matt McFerron and Daniel Ray have established a community-favorite neighborhood bar that focuses on classic cocktails, craft beers, and Old World wines along with a well-rounded whiskey list. It has also been named Athens Favorite Bar for Specialty Drinks for two years in a row by Flagpole readers.

As of this printing, no drink named a "Stiff One" could be found on Old Pal's extensive cocktail list. That being said, if you do pass by, tell them Ray sent you and see what happens.

ATHHALF

The Athens Half Marathon is a fundraiser organized annually by AthFest Educates in order to sustain and build the high-quality music and arts programs in the Athens community. Averaging 2,000 participants per race, AthHalf has become a highlight of the active Athens fall season.

AthHalf offers an exciting, albeit tiring, tour of Athens: historic neighborhoods, Sanford Stadium, and several landmarks of Athens musical history. Maybe hold out for the second water station for your refill though.